Where Has Grandma Gone?

A Child Learns About Alzheimer's Disease

Anne F. Butler

To order additional copies of this book, contact:
Xlibris
1-888-795-4274
www.Xlibris.com
Orders@Xlibris.com

INTRODUCTION

As a mental health therapist contracted at a nursing home and rehab for thirteen years, I had the opportunity to observe the reactions of children visiting a loved one. My clients were those with mental health issues, various kinds of dementia, and Alzheimer's disease. Most of them would spend the rest of their lives there.

It was especially disturbing to see the responses or lack of responses of the children visiting Alzheimer's patients. It was so obvious that they did not understand the change in their loved one, and it made them fearful. Also, the patient, most often a grandparent, would be disturbed that the child did not respond to them as they remembered.

It was even more disturbing to a child as their loved one moved through the more advanced stages of Alzheimer's.

Due to my concern for these children, I wanted to write a story that would help them understand Alzheimer's disease and dispel their fear. *Where Has Grandma Gone?* is a story to be read by the child. Later pages will contain information for the adult reader.

The writing of this book has been my dream for many years as I've seen the need for such a book. My prayer is that this book will be of great value to all those having to deal with Alzheimer's disease.

May God bless the readers and strengthen them in all their ways.

Sammy woke up so excited! Today was Saturday; he was going to spend the weekend with his grandma. His clothes and toys were all together, ready to go; he did that last night. It was going to be a good day! He had so much fun at Grandma's. Sammy was ready to go right after breakfast.

Mom came into the room, saying breakfast was ready. She looked upset that all his things were ready to go. Then she told him some very bad news: Grandma didn't live in her house anymore, so he can't go.

"Oh no! What? How can this be?" Sammy began to cry. "Where has Grandma gone? Mom, where has my grandma gone?"

Sammy didn't understand. Why would his grandma move from her nice house? He didn't want her to leave her house. He loved her house. Grandma didn't tell Sammy anything about her moving. Her house was Sammy's most fun place to go.

"Grandma says I'm her special grandchild. We are best friends. I know she would have told me if she were moving." Sammy asked again, "Where has my grandma gone?"

Mom didn't answer; she looked as if she was going to cry. She told Sammy she had something in the oven and went to the kitchen with the feeling that Sammy needed some time to think about the bad news.

Memories flooded Sammy's mind as he thought about Grandma's house. His mom and aunts said her house was an old, old house, and they laughed about it. But her house was Sammy's favorite place to be.

He thought about her front porch, so sunny in the morning and shady in the afternoon. That was Grandma's favorite place to sit. She would watch Sammy and his friends play in the yard. "Oh no!" Sammy worried. "What will Grandma do if she can't sit on her front porch anymore?"

Sammy thought about her garden with the radishes and tomatoes. Then, grinning, he remembered almost eating a little green worm climbing out of a tomato, which made Grandma laugh.

"Oh no!" Sammy cried. "Who will take care of Grandma's garden if I can't be there? She has a flower garden too, and I'm the one who waters it. I've gotta know, where has Grandma gone?"

There were so many interesting things at Grandma's house. She had an old, old wooden box on her back porch that was about to fall apart. She said she kept it because it belonged to her grandmother, and it was used a long time ago like a refrigerator to hold big chunks of ice. It reminded Grandma of when she was a little girl and would scrape off ice and eat it. Sammy said he'd like to do that too.

"The box is no good now"—Sammy laughed—"except to hide behind when we play hide-and-seek. Grandma always keeps special treats in her real refrigerator, and there are always Popsicles."

Sammy's favorite room was the back bedroom with its big comfortable bed. It was his whenever he spent the night. "Oh no!" Sammy cried with more tears, thinking that if Grandma didn't live there, he couldn't go spend the night. "Oh, where are you, Grandma? Why have you gone? Why didn't you tell me?"

Then Sammy remembered Grandma's bathroom with the big tub with feet, which made him so sad; he always took a bath before bedtime. It was like being in a swimming pool. "Oh, Grandma, will I ever be able to bathe in your tub again?"

In Grandma's living room, there was a fireplace with a mantel and a clock sitting on it that chimed each hour. Sammy loved to hear the chimes whenever he spent the night and wished they had a chiming clock at his house.

Sammy remembered how the whole family would come to Grandma's house for Sunday dinner. Grandma could make the best biscuits, and her fried chicken was "yum-yum" good. Sometimes Sammy helped with the meal. His cousins would be there too, and Sammy wondered if the cousins knew Grandma was gone. "Oh, Grandma, where have you gone? Why have you gone?"

There were more tears when Sammy thought about all the friends that he might not see ever again. They all loved playing in Grandma's front yard and backyard, where they could play soccer. Someday Sammy wanted to be on a soccer team like his brother.

Sammy said, "When Mom comes back to my room, I have to know right then where my grandma has gone and why she had to leave. I don't care about any breakfast."

When Mom returned, she looked sad, and Sammy knew she'd been crying. He knew she would miss Grandma too. She spent a lot of time at Grandma's house, helping with laundry and other things needed. Now there would be no need for her to go to Grandma's house. Sammy cried again and hugged Mom; they sat close on the side of the bed and both cried.

"Grandma has Alzheimer's disease, Sammy," Mom said, "and cannot live alone anymore. She's been taking pills, but it hasn't helped."

Sammy replied, "I've never heard of that disease. It must be terrible."

Sammy asked if children could catch it like strep or flu, and Mom said no. It was an adult disease. Sammy felt better about that, but then he asked if Mom and Dad could catch it. Mom explained that they were going to do all they could to keep from getting it. His brother and sister could not catch it because they, like Sammy, were not adults.

Mom explained that Alzheimer's is a brain disease—that the brain is a muscle and one must keep it exercised so it will be healthy. Sammy asked if riding his bike was a good brain exercise, and Mom said it was because one had to work to keep his balance and one was thinking while riding. She suggested that playing mental games like on the computer where one had to really think how to win were good. Schoolwork was especially good.

Sammy then said that his dad's jigsaw puzzle that he was working on was good; Mom agreed. Sammy said he would help Dad and that would exercise his brain too.

Mom added that playing a musical instrument, memorizing Bible verses and songs, and for adults, taking a course in college were wonderful brain exercises. Then Mom asked Sammy if he'd like to take guitar lessons. Sammy almost jumped for joy. "Oh, Mom, I'd love that!" Mom said they'd take care of that right away. She reminded Sammy that he already had memorized songs that he and Grandma sang and Bible verses he'd learned. This pleased Sammy.

Sammy was still worried about Grandma and asked, "Couldn't someone go live with Grandma? I'd love to go live with her." Mom said that wouldn't work.

"Why, Mom? I could do a lot of things to help her."

Then Mom said, "Grandma needs special help that we couldn't give her."

Sammy said, "It must be the doctor kind of help." Mom said it was.

Sammy told Mom, "Grandma didn't seem sick, and she looked healthy the last time I was there. She did forget where her plates went once, but I showed her where she kept them. Then she seemed okay."

Mom told Sammy why Grandma couldn't live alone. "When someone has Alzheimer's, they can't think like they used to," she said. "People with Alzheimer's get mixed up. Sometimes they don't even know where they are and don't know who their family members are."

Sammy remembered one day when Grandma couldn't remember a friend's phone number, and he had to look it up for her. One day, Grandma asked Sammy what month it was. Sammy assured Mom, "Grandma may not remember others and other things . . . but she'd never forget me. And she's got to remember her beautiful house." Sammy began to get angry, stomped his foot, and said how he hated this strange disease that had taken his grandma away from him. "I hate it! I hate it!"

Where did this awful disease come from? Mom said she had read that it was discovered by a doctor named Alois Alzheimer way back in 1906. Sammy again stomped his foot and said, "I wish he'd never discovered it, and I wish my grandma hadn't caught it."

Mom said, "Grandma didn't catch Alzheimer's. It's not a disease you can catch. Doctors don't know a lot about the disease right now and how you get it, but they have people studying it to learn more. It's not contagious."

Sammy told Mom he was sure Grandma would soon get better and not have Alzheimer's anymore and move back to her nice house. Then Sammy felt more hopeless when Mom told him a person can't get over Alzheimer's; one can have it forever.

"Oh no! You don't get well? Poor Grandma!" a gloomy Sammy moaned.

Sammy asked, "How did Grandma know she had this disease?" Mom said Grandma didn't really know she had Alzheimer's.

"Our doctor discovered Grandma's Alzheimer's when her short-term memory was leaving her. Short-term memory is the kind of remembering things that happened recently."

Mom said the brain may have already been in an early stage of Alzheimer's as far back as twenty years ago before the doctor could tell a person has the disease.

Hearing this made Sammy think about the time when Grandma couldn't remember where she put her eyeglasses and couldn't remember that she needed to wear them. "I found them for her in the kitchen, and she put them on. Another time, I found them in a bedroom drawer," he said with a big grin. Mom remembered one day when Grandma had lost her shoes and couldn't find them.

Due to Grandma's memory loss, the doctor had said she needed special care—someone to bathe and dress her—and that there were special homes that could accommodate her.

Sammy became sadder thinking of Grandma having to have help because she always helped him. He asked Mom, "Can I go help Grandma where she's living now?" Mom said she was in a special home where she had nurses and other helpers to take good care of her. Mom said she was proud of him for offering to help Grandma. This pleased Sammy.

According to Alzheimer's experts, it's very important for people with the disease to eat and drink enough. "The medical staff where Grandma is living will make sure she has good food," Mom assured Sammy. "Even if she says she's not hungry, they'll encourage her to eat." Sammy was upset hearing this. "Why, she can't even cook for herself? Not even her chicken or biscuits? I know she won't like that!"

Sammy agreed that Grandma was in a good place with helpers. "I still don't understand this awful disease, and I know Grandma will miss being away from her house. But could we go visit her?" Mom said yes. They could go shortly after breakfast.

By now, Sammy had made up his mind that he wanted to know all about this strange disease. Mom said they could learn together. "I don't know all about it either. When we learn all about Alzheimer's, it will help us understand about Grandma and why she has gone."

"Mom, I'm ready for breakfast!"

During their breakfast, Mom shared what she knew about Alzheimer's. She said she read that with Alzheimer's, the brain would shrink, and Sammy asked how a brain could shrink. Mom showed him a book with a picture of a brain with Alzheimer's and a normal brain. Sure enough, there was a shrunken brain and a normal brain. "Gross! That's weird." Sammy groaned.

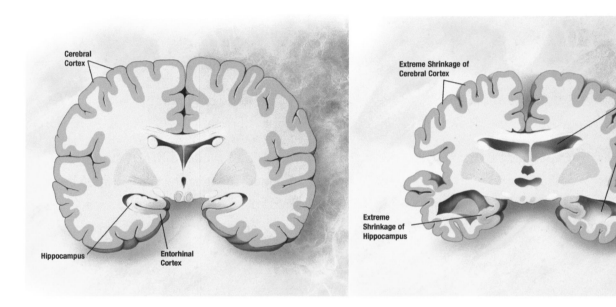

The book told that when the brain shrinks, many things a person has stored in their brain is erased; it's like tearing up a dictionary and all the words are gone or like erasing a dry-erase board that had something important written on it and now it was gone.

Sammy thought that was awful! "Oh no, Grandma may not even remember how to make her delicious biscuits or fry her chicken."

The book explained that the brain has three main parts: the cerebrum, the cerebellum, and the brain stem. These control everything that goes on in the body. When brain cells die, they are not replaced, causing the brain to shrink. Proteins, called plaques and tangles, build up in the brain, causing problems with everything the brain does.

Sometimes a person with Alzheimer's will act like a little baby, even forgetting how to eat and drink and do things like brushing their teeth. They need help doing all the little things they used to do for themselves. Sammy didn't like to think of his grandma being like a baby but said he was glad she had helpers. "I wish I could help."

Mom told about special things Grandma could do at the home if she felt like it. There were people who would come to entertain so they wouldn't get bored. Sammy said that was good because Grandma did a lot at her house. She planted vegetables and flowers and did a lot of cooking. Sometimes she put food into jars and called it canning.

Mom told Sammy people with Alzheimer's get tired easily, and Grandma might be napping when they go visit. "So we'll have to ask if it's okay to wake her."

Sammy said, "I hope she's awake. I can't wait to see where my grandma has gone. When we go visit Grandma, I'm going to tell her how much I love her cooking, and Mom can make biscuits like hers." Sammy asked if Grandma could talk to him, and Mom said she could still talk, but the part of the brain that controls speaking had been "messed up." This causes people to forget the right words to say. Mom said she knew that deep down in her heart, Grandma loved Sammy even if she couldn't say so.

Mom went on to say, "Grandma's hearing is okay even though she wears hearing aids, but her brain may not let her understand what you say to her. We must be patient and loving. The book says that when Grandma acts differently, we must remember that it's not Grandma. It's the Alzheimer's acting. It changes a person's personality, temper, and behavior."

Sammy said he had never seen Grandma act mean or ugly or say bad things. "She doesn't even have a temper! I don't like this Alzheimer's one bit! I'll just love Grandma and tell her we love her even if she doesn't act right."

Mom said, "Grandma has taken care of us for a long time, and now it's our turn to take care of her." Sammy said, "That's what I want to do."

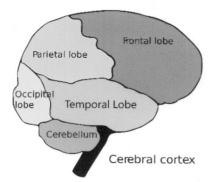

Mom went on to explain that the brain is divided into four parts called lobes. She touched the front of Sammy's head, telling him, "This is where the frontal lobe is located, and it has certain areas it controls, like movement and speech." Touching the top of Sammy's head, she said, "This is where the parietal lobe is located, and it gives us the ability to read, write, and do math."

Touching both sides of Sammy's head, Mom said, "This is where the temporal lobes are located. The left lobe helps us understand when someone is talking to us and helps us memorize. The right lobe gives us musical abilities and understanding of foreign languages. The occipital lobe is located at the lower back of the head." Sammy put his hand on this area. Mom said, "This lobe is responsible for vision and recognizing colors."

Sammy thought all this was interesting and said, "Wow! The brain is really special!"

"Grandma loves music!" he exclaimed. "We sing some silly songs together and some of the hymns from church. I'm gonna sing to Grandma when we go visit. I'll sing 'The Puffa-Billy' song and 'Amazing Grace.' I might teach her a new song we learned in Sunday school about Zacchaeus, a wee little man who climbed up in a tree to see Jesus. She'll love that song."

With breakfast finished, Sammy was ready to go see Grandma. "I'm so excited to see where my Grandma has gone!"

"There's more of the book that needs to be read," Mom said. "I'm going to keep it handy so even Dad can know about Alzheimer's."

"I can't wait to go see Grandma and give her some love," Sammy smiled. "Wow! After I see her, I'll understand all I need to know about Alzheimer's and why she had to leave her house. When I see Grandma, I'll say to her, 'So this is where you have gone!' Mom, I'm ready to go."

At last, it was time to go visit Grandma. Mom read a chapter in the book last night that had helped her understand what they needed to know before the visit. The drive to Grandma's new home was a short one; soon they parked in front of this large building. Sammy immediately said, "This doesn't look like a house." Mom said it was a special building that's called a home. Sammy wasn't sure he wanted to go inside, but he knew he had to go in if he wanted to visit Grandma.

Inside, a pretty lady sitting at a desk asked if she could help and Mom told her who we wanted to see. She said Grandma was sitting in the lobby. When Sammy saw her, she looked at him and held out her arms for a hug. She held him close and said she loved him. Sammy said, "I knew she wouldn't forget me—Mom, she knows me!"

Sammy and Mom had a good visit with Grandma and sang some songs together. When it was time for her lunch, they told her goodbye and said that they'd be back soon. Mom held Grandma's hand and prayed for her, and then they left.

In the car, Sammy told Mom that Grandma looked okay and would soon be back at her own house. Mom said, "Sammy, I'm so sorry, but Grandma is suffering from Alzheimer's and needs to stay at this place."

Hearing this made Sammy so angry! "Why! Why did my grandma get taken away from me?" Sammy couldn't help it; he cried. Mom held him close till he could stop the tears.

Mom said, "We'll continue to visit and love Grandma even when she's not okay. Grandma needs our love."

And Sammy said, "I need her love too!"

Later in the week was a sad day; Grandma's house was sold. Now someone else would be living in Grandma's beautiful house. One good thing, though, the people who bought the house didn't want the old icebox. They gave it to Sammy, and the chiming clock was given to Mom. Now Sammy had a special thing to remember from Grandma's house, and he had a chiming clock at his house. "Now I can remember Grandma forever!" Sammy smiled.

The next time they visited Grandma, she wasn't alone in the lobby. Others were with her, and they were all in wheelchairs. This bothered Sammy. "Grandma doesn't need a wheel chair, she can walk good."

Grandma seemed surprised to see them. Sammy wasn't sure she felt well. She didn't talk to Sammy or Mom like she did last visit. Sammy told her how he loved her house and all the fun they had. She smiled at Sammy but still was quiet. Sammy was careful not to let her know her house had been sold. At the end of their visit, Sammy gave Grandma a big hug and told her how much he loved her. Grandma hugged Sammy too, and Sammy said, "See, Mom, she still remembers me."

On the way home, Sammy told Mom that he thought Grandma wasn't feeling well, and Mom agreed. Mom said, "When you have a disease like Alzheimer's, there'll be times when you're not feeling well, but we can be happy that Grandma's in a special place where there's help for her."

During their next visit, late in the afternoon, Grandma was in her room. Sammy immediately said, "I don't like this room. It's cold and unfriendly, not like her beautiful house." Grandma was quiet, but Sammy talked to her and sang a song. Grandma listened but didn't sing with Sammy. Before they left, Sammy gave her a big hug and a kiss on her cheek. Grandma smiled and held Sammy's hand while Mom prayed. Sammy was so pleased.

In the car, Sammy talked about not liking Grandma's room, but Mom said it was okay. She said, "It has everything in it that Grandma needs—a bed with nice linens, a dresser with drawers, a closet, a chair, and a bathroom."

Sammy still didn't like it, but he said, "I'd like to bring some pictures to hang on her walls, especially some family pictures that would help Grandma remember." Mom agreed and said they could bring Grandma's special chair next visit also.

They took Grandma's chair and pictures next visit. Sammy hung the pictures. Grandma sat down in the chair quickly and seemed so pleased. Sammy had a surprise for Grandma. He had a new guitar and had had two lessons already. He wanted to show this to Grandma, but she didn't show much interest in it.

Even though this was a disappointment to Sammy, it was still a good visit. Mom prayed for Grandma, and she smiled at Sammy. But they were not sure Grandma knew exactly who they were.

Summer had gone too quickly, and there was a feeling of fall in the air. Last visit, Sammy was glad when Grandma noticed the pretty leaves outside her window. Sammy reminded her of how they had raked leaves into a big pile and Sammy would jump in it and get all covered with leaves. Sammy laughed when he remembered. To his surprise, Grandma smiled and then laughed. Sammy was thrilled to see Grandma laugh. But Sammy wasn't sure she really remembered. Sammy sang the "Zaccheus" song to her, and she smiled again. Today was another good visit.

In the car, Sammy said, "Did you see Grandma laugh when I laughed?"

Some days, their visits seemed the same, with Grandma getting weaker and weaker. She didn't talk much, but one day, she remembered Sammy's name. That was the first time she'd called his name. She never spoke Mom's name. Sammy told Mom, "I told you she's getting better." Mom smiled but didn't say anything. This visit, Sammy tried laughing again, but Grandma didn't laugh anymore.

Several days later, when they visited, Grandma was in what they called an activity. Several others were with her, listening to a group of singers. The music seemed a little loud to Sammy, and he knew Grandma didn't like loud music. When Grandma saw them, she tried to roll her wheelchair out of the room. Sammy saw she needed help, so he rolled the wheelchair for her. Sammy and Grandma seemed to like this. He told Grandma he was learning to play some of their songs on his guitar, but she didn't seem to understand. Mom prayed for Grandma, and they left her sitting quietly in her room. This was not a real good visit.

Sammy would have a birthday in two weeks, but Grandma wouldn't be able to come. That was sad because Grandma always baked the birthday cake. Sammy said, "I guess Grandma doesn't even know I'll be a year older."

Sammy's birthday was good though because he got a sweet little puppy for his gift. Sammy named him Jack. Jack was going to visit Grandma as soon as Mom got permission from the home.

The permission was given, and Jack went for a visit. Grandma loved Jack! This was the happiest Grandma had been in a long time. Jack loved Grandma too; he snuggled in her lap and looked happy. This was a fun visit.

On their next visit, Dad came with them. He talked to Grandma but looked worried and soon left to wait for them in the car. Sammy's brother and sister wouldn't come to see Grandma. They wanted to just remember her like the last time they had seen her. Mom and Sammy had their usual visit with Sammy's songs and Mom's prayers. It was a good visit. Grandma said Jack was a good dog.

Sammy was a year older. He tried to tell Grandma all about his birthday, but Grandma didn't seem to be listening. Sammy told Mom he thought Grandma's memory was getting worse. Mom said she thought so also.

Mom and Sammy learned it was better to visit early in the day. Grandma seemed to feel better then. Late in the afternoon, Grandma seemed to be acting out. The nurse said this acting out is called sundowners. It happens late in the afternoon, and strangely enough, it also happens when there is a full moon. Sammy thought this was weird.

On one visit, Grandma was in her wheelchair in the lobby when they arrived. She didn't pay much attention when they greeted her, but suddenly, Grandma got very angry and tried to hit Mom. "That's not my Grandma! My Grandma has never been angry or mean." Sammy began to cry. He couldn't believe what he was seeing; even Jack seemed frightened. Mom told him, "Stop that crying. That will not help Grandma."

Sammy rolled Grandma to her room. Mom sat on the side of the bed and talked softly to Grandma. Sammy carefully moved closer to Grandma, and she let him take her hand. Sammy told Grandma how much he loved her and began to softly sing "Amazing Grace." Soon Grandma was calm. Both of them prayed for her, and when they left, Grandma looked as if she was getting sleepy.

Both Mom and Sammy had a lot of talking to do about this visit. Mom explained to Sammy what she had read about this behavior in the book. She told him how there are seven stages of Alzheimer's, and Grandma was moving through them. In stage 4, they may express their feelings by acting out. Grandma might be feeling sad and didn't know how to express her feelings except like she did this visit. Mom said, "Even when Grandma acts in a strange way, we'll still love her."

Sammy said, "I'll have to think about this Alzheimer's acting. I hate it! I hate it!"

After Grandma getting so angry at Mom, Sammy was a little worried about their next visit. When they arrived, Sammy noticed something and asked Mom, "Shouldn't Grandma be wearing her glasses and hearing aids?" Mom said yes.

They couldn't find them at first. Then they were found in Grandma's closet in the pocket of a dress. Grandma didn't seem to want to wear them, so they put them in her dresser drawer where they'd be safe. Grandma was pleasant this visit. Sammy played his guitar for her, but then Grandma started saying some strange things about her family they knew were not true. They didn't tell her she was wrong; they just let Grandma talk. They listened and nodded their heads so she would know they were listening. This was the first time Grandma had talked this much. Grandma held Jack on her lap the whole time.

The next visit was surprising because Grandma was not in her room. Her wheelchair was empty; her clothes, shoes, and all her things were piled on her bed. There were empty drawers and an empty closet. What was happening to Grandma? Mom found a nurse's aide and asked, "Where has Grandma gone?" Mom was told that Grandma had started wandering a great deal now, up and down the halls.

Then they saw Grandma coming, carrying several of her dresses and seeming confused to see them. Sammy ran to her, but she didn't want a hug and pushed him away. She looked at Sammy like she didn't know who he was. This hurt Sammy's feelings, making him want to cry. Then he remembered Mom saying not to cry. Sammy walked beside her, being careful not to get too close. Mom had told him several times that an Alzheimer's patient has a personal space, and they must give you permission to enter. Sammy began to tell her he loved her, then she reached out her hand and they walked together like friends. Grandma had given Sammy permission to enter her personal space.

They went to Grandma's room to put all the things back where they belonged. The nurse came in and said Grandma was having a problem with wandering and not sleeping well, but this was typical with Alzheimer's, and they were taking care of it.

The nurse said it was good that Grandma was in a home because if she had been in her own home, she might have wandered outside and put herself in danger. Sammy said he was glad Grandma was safe.

Mom thanked the nurse and said to let her know if they needed anything. On the way home, Mom told Sammy what she felt Grandma was doing. She said, "This behavior usually happens in stage 5. If the Alzheimer's patient worked before retirement, they'd sometimes remember they worked and try to dress for work." Mom felt Grandma was remembering that she was a secretary before retiring and was trying to find her work clothes. "She must have remembered that she used to have somewhere to go and needed to dress for work."

Sammy said, "I'm proud of Grandma remembering her job. That means she's getting better." Mom didn't reply.

Sammy was having a graduation in three days. He was excited but sad because his best friend, Grandma, would not be there. "Grandma probably doesn't even know I'm old enough to be graduating."

Winter arrived and Mom swapped out some of Grandma's clothes that were warmer. Grandma didn't recognize that these were her clothes. "I help Mom by putting Grandma's name in her clothes," Sammy said proudly. Grandma seemed to be feeling cold when they arrived. Since Jack was a bigger pup now, he was like a blanket when he was in Grandma's lap. She held him close; Jack liked Grandma's lap.

The visits were getting harder because they never knew how Grandma was doing. She was not the Grandma they remembered. Sometimes they felt like they didn't even know her. They continued to love her no matter how she acted. Sammy felt so sad for Grandma and hated the awful disease that had taken her away. Her brain had been so erased she couldn't remember all the wonderful times she shared with Sammy. But Sammy remembered, and that was why he continued to love her so much. Sammy said, "When she talks crazy, I'll just listen and say I love you."

They went to see Grandma two times that week because they were worried about how she was doing. When they walked into her room—what a surprise! Grandma was a mess! Her hair was in tangles. She wasn't wearing her glasses and shoes and had mismatched clothes on. A nurse's aide came into the room and said Grandma was resisting care. She wouldn't let her aide help her and was acting mean to her. Then Mom discovered that the aide was new, and Grandma was frightened of the change. "Changes upset Alzheimer's patients," Mom said. Mom talked softly to Grandma and sat beside her on the bed. She brushed her hair, put on her shoes, and washed her face and hands. Before they left, Mom requested that a familiar aide help with Grandma's care and reminded the aide that Grandma's privacy must be respected; some patients are very modest. They stayed a little longer, making sure Grandma was okay. Then both Mom and Sammy prayed and told her they loved her and left.

Christmas arrived, and they had snow. Sammy wished Grandma knew about the snow; she didn't listen when he told her. Sammy gave her a cute stuffed puppy that was like Jack for Christmas. Grandma loved the pup and cuddled it all the time. Sammy was thankful that Grandma didn't know the family couldn't go to her house for Christmas dinner. That would make her very sad. Everybody was sad too.

So many of their visits were hard now because Grandma didn't always seem to feel good. She always looked at them when they prayed though; they know God was hearing their prayers and letting Grandma know He was listening.

There was a concern because Grandma was refusing to eat. She would drink with help but didn't ask for it. That really worried Mom and Sammy. Sammy wondered if Grandma would like a Popsicle. He remembered how they enjoyed Popsicles at Grandma's house.

They had a new year. It had been such a long time since Grandma was in this special home, and she was not getting any better. Sammy now knew that Grandma would never leave this home. He was glad she had doctors and nurses to care for her; she could no longer care for herself at all. Sometimes she was afraid of them whenever they visited. Mom reminded Sammy to get permission for a hug. She didn't like anyone close to her. When walking, she would hold her head down, looking at the floor. Mom now felt Grandma was in stage 5.

On one visit, Sammy brought a Popsicle for Grandma. She wasn't sure what he was giving her, but she took a taste and seemed to like it. Together they both finished their popsicles. Sammy was so pleased! It worried them when they talked to Grandma. She would listen, but they were never sure she understood. Today she looked at Sammy when he sang; he was so pleased. "Oh, Grandma, how I love you!"

The next visit was scary! Grandma was sitting on her bed, crying. Mom asked her what was wrong, and she said, "This bad man's in my room. He's gonna get me and carry me away." She was so scared she was shaking. Then Mom and Sammy noticed the TV was on with a scary movie. Mom turned off the TV, and Grandma let Mom hold her tight. Sammy put his arms around her too and said, "We're not going to let anyone hurt you." The nurse came into the room and said Grandma had a spell of paranoia, which can be very scary. The nurse suggested we just leave the TV unplugged. Mom reached over and unplugged it.

On the way home, Mom talked about how they must think about the time when Grandma wouldn't be with them anymore. This made Sammy very sad. He said, "I can see how the Grandma I love so much is disappearing, but my love will never disappear."

Last night, the nurse called to say Grandma had fallen and was taken to the hospital with a broken hip. Oh no! Poor Grandma! They went to the hospital to check on Grandma. She didn't look good; they didn't stay very long. Grandma was sleeping from the medicine they had given her. Grandma had to stay in the hospital for two weeks because she would not eat, and she developed pneumonia. Sammy and Mom went to the home for a visit after she was out of the hospital; she still didn't look good. Mom and Sammy prayed a special prayer before they left. They asked God to heal Grandma.

Since Grandma was back at the home, their visits were getting further and further apart. Sometimes, a visit seemed to bother Grandma, and she seemed sad. Often, she was so quiet and didn't talk at all. She surprised them on one visit because she asked them, "Where am I?" Mom and Sammy didn't really know how to answer; how could they tell her in a way she would understand? But then she seemed to forget she asked. Grandma sat in her chair and didn't even try to walk; the hip must still bother her. Sammy said, "Oh, Grandma, I wish I could help you." The nurse came into the room and said Grandma was sleeping better. They were glad to hear that. Sammy sang "Jesus Loves Me" to Grandma, and then they prayed and left.

A really bad thing happened in the next visit. When Mom walked into the room, Grandma yelled at her, "That's my purse! You stole my purse!" Mom didn't know what to do; it was the same purse Mom always carried. Mom stood still for a moment then put the purse out of sight and talked calmly to Grandma about how she was feeling. Grandma became calm, and Sammy was able to move close to her and told Grandma he needed a hug. Sammy was so pleased when she gave him a hug. "Wow, that was great!" Before they left, Sammy sang "Jesus Loves Me," and Grandma hummed along with him.

It had now been another year with Grandma at the home. Their visits had gone okay most of the time, but there were times when Grandma didn't even seem to know they were there. Jack didn't even interest her at times.

Sammy had been busy with school and had not been able to spend as much time with Grandma as he would like. Now that the weather was pleasant, he and Jack sometimes walked to the home. Sometimes Grandma would love Jack, and there were other times when she didn't seem to notice him. This was so sad.

On one visit, a nurse asked Sammy what he wanted to be when he got out of school. He told her, "I'm going to be a doctor or a scientist and get rid of this Alzheimer's disease for good!"

Sammy started to read Grandma's favorite Bible verses to her. This helped her; he could tell she enjoyed this. Sometimes she even had a smile on her face. Sammy felt one verse from Proverbs was for him: "A merry heart doeth good like a medicine" (Proverbs 17:22 KJV). Sammy felt he had not been very merry lately.

Grandma was sleepy most of the time. She would nap with Jack on her lap, or Jack would lay beside her if she were in her bed. Sammy still sang to her and played his guitar. He was quite a musician now. Even though Grandma didn't talk to Mom and Sammy, they still visited because they loved her so much. She was still Sammy's special grandma.

One visit really worried them because Grandma was asleep in her bed when they arrived. She had not been taking naps in her bed; she just napped in her chair. Sammy said, "Oh no! What does this mean? Is Grandma getting worse?" The nurse told them that Grandma was sleeping more and more in the daytime. She didn't seem to be able to walk, and eating was still a big problem. Mom asked if there was anything they could do, and the nurse said this was the natural progression of Alzheimer's and they just had to let it take its course. "Oh no! That's so sad!" Sammy said. "I want to help Grandma. I want to help her."

Mom said this was explained in the book; she kept it handy. The information in the book kept her up-to-date with Grandma's progress or lack of progress. Mom felt Grandma was now entering stage 7, which was the last stage. Her actions in this stage resembled those of a two-year-old child. At this stage, music and touch were good for communication. They stayed a little longer, and Sammy held Grandma's hand and sang softly to her. She was peaceful and still, so they prayed and left. Sammy was very troubled.

On the way home, Mom and Sammy were quiet, both troubled. "Are we losing Grandma?" Sammy asked. Mom said they would never lose Grandma because she would always be in their hearts. Mom reminded Sammy of all the beautiful, precious memories they had of her and how no one could take those away from them. Mom said, "We will still visit with Grandma and talk to her even if we don't know if she understands. We will still pray with her, and you, Sammy, will still sing all the wonderful songs you know. We will love Grandma till the end of her days. Grandma has lived a wonderful life, and you have helped to make her life wonderful by the love you give her." As Sammy thought about what Mom was saying, his joy of having such a special Grandma returned, and he smiled as he said, "Grandma and I are going to be okay!"

LEARNING ABOUT ALZHEIMER'S

This section is for the adult reader. Information is provided by the author from her many years of experience as a mental health therapist working with Alzheimer's and other dementia patients and the Alzheimer's Association.

I will mention a word of hope. The symptoms of Alzheimer's can be treated with love and understanding that will help them to have a better quality of life. I have personally seen this happen. Your care can make a difference.

CASE HISTORY—ALOIS ALZHEIMER

"She sits on the bed with a helpless expression. What is your name? Auguste. Last name? Auguste. What is your husband's name? Auguste, I think. Your husband? Ah, my husband. She looks as if she didn't understand the question."

So opens the first entry in a long-lost file of a woman identified only as Auguste D. The interview occurred November 26, 1901, and the physician was neuropsychiatrist Alois Alzheimer. Alzheimer described Auguste's symptoms as progressive cognitive impairment, hallucinations, delusions, and psychosocial incompetence. He observed her until her death in 1906.

That year, Alzheimer described what he found in Auguste's brain during autopsy, including neurofibrillary tangles, cortical shrinkage, and plaque buildup between neurons. It was the first description of what became known as Alzheimer's disease. (National Geographic, a User's Guide, Special Issue, January 2019)

STATISTICS

Statistics from the Alzheimer's Association 2018 report the following:

a. More than five million Americans are living with Alzheimer's disease. There may be many more that are not reported.

b. Alzheimer's disease is the only cause of death among the top ten in America that cannot be prevented, cured, or even slowed.

c. Every sixty-five seconds, someone in the US develops Alzheimer's or other dementia.

d. There are more deaths from Alzheimer's disease than from other major diseases such as heart disease, stroke, and HIV.

e. Alzheimer's disease is the sixth leading cause of death in the US. One in three seniors die from Alzheimer's disease or other dementia.

f. Women and African Americans are twice as likely to develop Alzheimer's. Hispanics are 1.5 times as likely.

g. Education, income, and where you live surprisingly plays a role in Alzheimer's.

h. Almost two-thirds of Americans with Alzheimer's disease are women.

i. Since 2000, deaths from Alzheimer's disease have increased by 89 percent.

RESEARCH

Today no cause or cure has yet been found. But many areas of research give hope that there will be a cure.

The Alzheimer's Association states that among all Americans alive today, if those who will get Alzheimer's disease were diagnosed in the mild cognitive stage—before dementia—it would collectively save $7 trillion to $7.9 trillion in health and long-term care costs. So you can see why research is so important.

Research is being done regarding the question, Is Alzheimer's a genetic disease? Can specific genes be passed down through a family lineage that would be a risk for Alzheimer's?

Information from the September/October 2018 *Saturday Evening Post* reports the number of genes known to cause Alzheimer's has moved from four to more than forty since 1977.

According to the Alzheimer's Disease Research (a BrightFocus Foundation program), an estimated one in twenty people with Alzheimer's have the early-onset form, which is clinically apparent by age sixty. The most common form is late-onset Alzheimer's (LOAD) where symptoms become apparent after age sixty. In their research, they have identified a number of genes playing a role in the development of Alzheimer's. But the exact role of these genes is still being determined. This study may increase resistance to the development of Alzheimer's disease.

A recent study has indicated that improving brain blood flow can improve the cognitive function of Alzheimer's patients. With a grant from Alzheimer's Disease Research, Dr. Chris Schaffer of Cornell University is in the process of screening drugs that could alleviate the cause of the blood flow reduction.

Alzheimer's Disease Research is the key funder of EyesOnALZ, the first-ever crowdsourced project to engage the public in Alzheimer's research. The project (fall 2018) hit a major milestone by exceeding ten thousand volunteers, citizen scientists, joining in to help speed up the time-consuming data analysis of stalled blood vessels in the brain.

With the support from Alzheimer's Disease Research, Louisiana scientist Robert Newton, PhD, is conducting a clinical trial on the effects of physical activity on the dementia risk for older African Americans.

John Hopkins University Medical Center (Baltimore, Maryland) and the National Institute on Aging are doing a study related to hearing loss being linked to Alzheimer's.

Some researchers now believe a cluster of diseases such as diabetes and heart disease may play a part. They know for sure that Alzheimer's disease is not caused simply by old age, (even though the possibility of developing Alzheimer's doubles in each decade after age sixty-five).

Dr. Peng Xu, the postdoctoral associate at the Fisher Center for Alzheimer's Research at the Rockefeller University in New York, is doing research on identifying novel pathways and targets for Alzheimer's disease. His present research focuses on neurotoxic amyloid beta, which is thought to play a key role in Alzheimer's. He is working to understand the cellular process.

Dr. Martin Farlow, clinical director and researcher at Indiana University's Department of Neurology in Indianapolis, said, "The accumulation of information during the past five to six years has taken us to a place where we can begin to unravel the puzzle and put the pieces together. We are making progress toward the ultimate goal—to treat people before they develop Alzheimer's symptoms—and will continue to do so in coming years."

> President Donald Trump recently signed the Building Our Largest Dementia Infrastructure for Alzheimer's Act (BOLD) bill, which authorizes $100 million over five years to develop a public health approach that will improve prevention, treatment and care for patients with Alzheimer's disease. This bill will help translate research into practice and lead to more effective interventions and treatments. (The Associated Press, January 6, 2019)

This bill outlines three primary avenues for action: (1) establishing centers of excellence in public health practice related to Alzheimer's disease, (2) increasing data related on the prevalence of Alzheimer's disease, and (3) creating cooperative agreement awards to strengthen Alzheimer's disease public health initiatives.

The bill authorizes funds to award organizations that execute evidence-based interventions related to education and communication about Alzheimer's and related dementias, early detection and diagnosis, mitigating potentially avoidable hospitalizations, improving caregiver and patient support, assisting with care planning and management, and assisting other activities as deemed appropriate.

Any health department awarded must furnish 30 percent of the funds specified in the agreement to execute the proposed activities.

A blood test to screen for Alzheimer's disease may help detect the disease before symptoms appear. The test designated by the US Food and Drug Administration as a breakthrough device may accelerate this tool's approval for use in health-care settings. The test was developed by Alzheimer's Disease Research grant recipients Phillip Verghese, PhD, and Joel Braunstein, MD, MBA, and previous grantees David Holtzman, MD, and Randall Bateman, MD. This highly sensitive test is expected to be cheaper and less invasive than the current screening options, allowing treatment to begin sooner.

We are hopeful the various studies will eventually find a cure for Alzheimer's and a reason for so many cases of dementia.

There is no medicine like hope, no incentive so great, no tonic so powerful as expectation of something better tomorrow. (Orison Marden, American Parkinson Disease Association)

HOW TO DELAY OR POSSIBLY PREVENT ALZHEIMER'S DISEASE

Remembering that the brain is a muscle that must be exercised to keep it healthy helps you choose activities that match that criteria.

Any brain-challenging games such as solitaire, crossword puzzles, word finds, jigsaw puzzles, etc. will help keep the brain sharp.

Having an interest in sports as an observer or a participant will keep your mind alert.

Using the computer, laptop, etc., reading a book, and anything that is mentally stimulating is great.

Having an active social life, traveling, doing something different.

Having a hobby, becoming a collector, being a bird-watcher.

Tending a vegetable or flower garden. Having a compost pile to tend.

You cannot be a stay-at-home person and expect to exercise your brain as it should be exercised. Have an interesting activity that will get you out of the house for a while.

Practice smiling and learn to laugh.

There is an argument that has gone on for years about whether aluminum may help cause Alzheimer's disease. I am of the opinion that there may be a connection because increased levels of aluminum have been found in the brain of Alzheimer's victims. Also, patients undergoing kidney dialysis often get dialysis dementia because the water used in kidney dialysis had high levels of aluminum. When rabbits are given high levels of aluminum, they get the same high levels in their brains as human Alzheimer's patients.

Right now, there is no hard scientific proof that aluminum can cause Alzheimer's disease, but if you want to play it safe, you may wish to limit your exposure to aluminum as much as possible. You can do this by limiting your use of cellular antacid tablets, processed foods, certain underarm deodorants, watching exposure to bentonite clay, aluminum pans, and drinking water high in aluminum. Get in the habit of reading labels.

This information was gathered from the Alzheimer's Disease Education and Referral Center (ADEAR).

CONTACT INFORMATION

For further information, you may contact the Alzheimer's Association at 225 N. Michigan Ave., Floor 17, Chicago, IL 60601 or call 1-800-272-3900. This is a 24-7 free help line.

To find the Alzheimer's Association anywhere in the United States, visit www.alz.org/findus.

For educational material, call the HELP line at 1-800-457-5679.

For information about participating in a Walk to End Alzheimer's, visit alz.org/walk.

To learn more about improving the response to Alzheimer's—the nation's largest under-recognized public health crisis—visit alz.org/advocacy.

To learn more about AAIC (Alzheimer's Association International Conference), visit alz.org/AAIC.

To be a partner in research, contact the Alzheimer's Disease Research, 22512 Gateway Center Drive, Clarksburg, MD 20871.

To order or print copies of publications, call 1-855-345-6237 or to download digital versions, visit www.brightfocus.org/publications. Resources are also available in Spanish.

For help in finding community resources and services in your local community, visit alz.org/CRF.

For donations, visit alz.org/augmatch.

To learn more about Parkinson's disease, visit apdaparkinson.org or call 1-800-223-2732.

> If I can stop one heart from breaking, if I can ease one life the aching or cool one pain, or help one lonely person into happiness again, I shall not live in vain. (Anonymous)

ABOUT THE AUTHOR

Anne F. Butler, MS, CVW
212 Adele Street, Rainbow City, AL 35906
afb56@bellsouth.net

Education: BS Education, Jacksonville (AL) State University
MS Counseling, Jacksonville (AL) State University
Special training: Dr. Richard Powers—Director, Alabama Bureau of Geriatric Psychiatry
Naomi Feil—Founder and Executive Director, Validation Training Institute

After teaching for eleven years from kindergarten through elementary and high school grades, Anne joined the staff of the Bridge, Alabama's largest state-funded residential substance abuse program for adult males, which would later include adult females. A few years later, an adolescent program for boys and girls would be added.

By having a teacher's degree, Anne moved from her work as a marriage and substance abuse counselor to that of a one-room schoolhouse teacher with eighteen students. Counseling and regular school work—grades 7 through 11—became her daily schedule for twenty years.

In the late 1990s, Anne changed careers; she was employed by the Mountain Lakes Behavioral Health Care, Guntersville, Alabama, as a geriatrics mental health therapist and spent the next thirteen years under contract at Attalla Health Care, a nursing home, in Attalla, Alabama.

During this time, she carried a caseload of thirty-two men and women, which included residents suffering from various forms of mental illness, depression, Alzheimer's disease, and other forms of dementia, plus dealing with the resulting behavior problems.

During Anne's years as a therapist—substance abuse, marriage counseling, foster parent for teens, and mental health—she was a sought-after speaker for in-service training and other engagements.

Anne has a sixty-three-year-long marriage to Harry. She is a mother of four, grandmother of fifteen, and great-grandma to nineteen (last count).

CPSIA information can be obtained
at www.ICGtesting.com
Printed in the USA
LVHW010253160519
618046LV00016B/452/P

9 781796 027808